SOME BUSINESS
RECENTLY TRANSACTED
IN THE WHITE WORLD

Some Business Recently Transacted in the White World by Edward Dorn

FRONTIER PRESS 1971

ACKNOWLEDGEMENTS: "C. B. & Q.," BLACK MOUNTAIN REVIEW #7 AND **The Moderns,** CORINTH BOOKS, NEW YORK, 1963, ED. LEROI JONES; "DRIVING ACROSS THE PRAIRIE," EVERGREEN REVIEW; "SOME BUSINESS RECENTLY TRANSACTED IN THE WHITE WORLD," LAMPETER MUSE.

COPYRIGHT © 1957 BY BLACK MOUNTAIN COLLEGE
COPYRIGHT © 1957, 1963, 1969, 1971 BY EDWARD DORN
COPYRIGHT © 1971 BY FRONTIER PRESS
STEWART STREET, WEST NEWBURY, MASS 01985
DESIGN BY RON CAPLAN

In speaking of what
is Outward and what
is Inward one refers
not to Place, but
to what is Known and what
is Not known

A NARRATIVE
WITH SCATTERED NOUNS   1

A EPIC   10

OF EASTERN NEWFOUNDLAND,
ITS INNS & OUTS   11

C. B. & Q.   26

THE TERRIFIK REFINERY
IN BIAFRA   38

DRIVING
ACROSS THE PRAIRIE   54

THE GARDEN OF BIRTH   66

THE SHERIFF
OF McTOOTH COUNTY,
KANSAS   68

GREENE
ARRIVES ON THE SET   77

SOME BUSINESS
RECENTLY TRANSACTED
IN THE WHITE WORLD   80

A Narrative
with Scattered Nouns

MY SOJOURN IN NEW ENGLAND had been full of a kind of random leisure. The shrine at Newburyport I visited three times and upon each occasion I threw pressed cakes into the pathways leading to the great roads. With my friends I kept a watch for the newly arrived paperbacks and eventually learned to discriminate between the pizza of two establishments. And quite soon we discovered an old fountain beneath the Greyhound bus stop. It proved possible, after a careful explanation, to get the priestess to turn a frappe into a true milkshake. But in the light of what follows these were trivial affairs. It is enough to say that during these first days we divided our ears between the false prophets of Harvard Square and the interglacial breezes of the northern coastal region.

Plum Island became one of our favorite haunts. The lightness of its air, the fairness of its granulation and the extreme openness to the seas who run home there. The lightness of its air. That is the way it is aspected. There is not a great amount of driftwood. What driftwood there is scattered near the sea grass is of a compelling nature. Its surface is possessed of a mild satin glow, an encircling gestalt which seems independent of stock solar light. It is otherwise farctate.

I believe it was on the occasion of our fifth return to the beach that our small group began in a splendid moment of mystery the building of a great sea charm some fifty feet in diameter several of whose vertical members rose to a height of twenty feet and which was of such simple unembellished power the pedestrians of that part of the shore gave it a wide berth and many fleeting glances. If none of the uninitiated stooped to kneel, it is equally true they were on that spot given the assurance that a prayer was under construction to alleviate the loathsome condition of their official sanity when the builders did on several gathering impulses create a crescendo of bows and threw themselves upon the salt margin, caught, mutatis mutandis, inside their sudden wish.

They wanted to call back the departing sun. Blood was not in their minds, blood was in their hearts, but these celebrants are removed a considerable distance from the altar of that center, tho not so far of course as the pedestrians. As everyone can feel, this is the nature of all true difference. There was a metaphysical space alternating them across what is taken to be the real space. They came across a seam of time which in some vast tongue of silence had been nearly joined. They had entered a process, at the instance of this Circle, in which the future took its tail in its mouth and clamped its teeth quite firmly into the flesh of the past. The past is not simply that, they knew, to find oneself in it is not a "predicament" and is never dismissed by an appeal to indecision. I meant to say torque, the result of the twisting of those time fragments we count one two three. I was among the processionals. The event was filmed and still exists, I believe, in a cardboard box.

This event occurred under the very eye of the scald. He took no formal notice because in fact he may not have known of it. Nonetheless I owe any granite sense I have of New England to him and refer at all times of doubt to the Chronicles which are the result of his labor. And I must say it was with some deeply lateral instinct the Charm was made a tribute to the Eye of the Scald.

The beginning was impulsive. In that moment, one of us, I have not kept a record of which, did grasp the first piece of salt wood and place it on its end — thereby creating on the skin of the earth a mark so abrupt and mad that the other pieces presented themselves as volunteers who had been waiting thruout encyclopaedic millenia for chance climate to end and they be seized by the agents of intelligence bearing no explanation whatever. This happened. They were found and came to life entirely uncompromised by growth and all the mute worry it can generate. The soul is here. There was no going back to that imagined moment before it is. It must arrive that way else one is stuck with a plan of the thing and invariable lapse, I mean wasn't that what the lapse was about, the Discussion. Even now I prefer green apples to red ones and for precisely that natural difference. However you might choose to appear, all the world knows you've no place to go. The simple fact occurred that the driftwood at that moment found something to do with these people. This had nothing at all to do with a late vulgarisation called "setting up a shrine". No names. Absolutely.

So they stopped talking and made a ring. It went up, into the nature of nature. The time shift was its own perceptual fulfillment. They did not have to try, in other words, did not have to be conscious that comprehension as such had conveniently gone to Florida forever. Bought a boat. Set up a cottage. Put on one of those funny caps with a sun visor with an emblem up front and which is, they say, a good thing to do with your mother. They were not, in any sense, to be compromised by chance. Not at the end of the sixth decade. A few decades back the whole thing could have been dismissed as a categorical impulse, a literary enlightenment, a piece of the late reconditioned romantic, or some more severely self-imposed economic mockery in which the leader is presumed to have given it all back to the Organizers without even a formal nod to God.

The Scholiast was present on the occasion of the return some days later to the finished circle. There was some uneasiness when this official was brought to survey the spot with the paraphenalia of his own particular eye. Members of this class will habitually look for a surrogate. Then they will sniff the air for a god. They are trying to locate the direction from which the permission came. But there had been no sacrifice. No Surrogate and no permission.

At least not in Public Light, but anyone might guess that given the date. And I'll have to admit what we had there was a slightly funky scholiast. He was as cool as he could manage under the circumstances. They were this: A shrine had been erected and existed at the desolate southern end of the public beach. There was still no means to determine if it had been noticed by the sea. And the aesthetics of the situation were so loose no one of the worshippers would have proposed a test. Permission can be violent, Rejection can be mild.

Thusia may be taken many ways. And result in anything. There were no sacra in evidence smaller than the natural conformation of the event in the sand and grass.

The gate of the edifice was to the Gulf of Maine. The circle was of late afternoon conception therefore any connection it might have had with the rising sun was left to co-incidence. The East Southeastern appointment kept the heat of an afternoon social movement. It is well known the urge to enter into a life of any form can get so wild the driver will aim his car straight up a tree and have something to tell the insurance adjustor.

What disturbed the Scholiast most was one feature of the shrine which came in with his presence. At this moment when the holy place seemed to become its own creation there washed ashore a green tree.

There is no way to name it without slipping into the mind killing error of description. It appeared a genetically prompted result of an Ash and an Elm, almost as if it were a parody of some dirty joke about democracy. An Elmish Seaash. It was quite definitely wind swept along its north-south axis, it followed in other words the string of its existence its arcing seemed less taken from its nature than from its experience. As it emerged from the sea it was of the utmost pale and refreshing green when one of the mystics seized it in the Thusia of the shrine's new energy and planted it as directly as feeling can locate into the sand in the magnetic center of the circle and the breeze straightway took its half cured leaves and rustled them, a completion so inaudible and bright the sound was in fact a level of a system not theretofore present upon the shore. My own feeling at that precise time was that Shu was not much pleased, but in some perfect laziness looking.

It must be understood that this is play. There is not even a shred of a work-ethic here. These people are beautifully ascended. They pay attention only to the ecstatic of the absolute and have no tolerance whatsoever for the static of the absolute. They have not interdicted the elements to seek a smaller location. Of course they are generally absent-minded. They remember the minded result, that it dries, or is wiped off with a handkerchief.

The Scholiast was doubtful, It was about the aetiology of the green tree he said. The flute must invent the fingers of its awakener, the Universe is as much a guitar as it is some drying excitement as to the manner in which it curves. They listened rapt with their mouth sprung open. One might question even the most spiritually pure and spontaneous of ones insights if they are of uncertain agent — Nice Weather for instance, is an intolerable comment. It is far more outrageous than murder.

And then the Scholiast turned annoyed toward the commotion which intervened between the mystics and the water. A collective had built a fire over which they tortured frankfurters into a state of black flesh and running juice. They ate their interestingly shaped kills with exaggerated teeth while their eyes bugged and probed the surroundings. The empty packages blew across the sand to advertise that their greed included two entire bodies of water, the Atlantic & Pacific, and a fact writ large, ALL PORK. What is this cannibalism? the Scholiast muttered. Janice has a weenie! the one called Martha screamed. All Meat! Janice shouted into the wind. Janice has a weenie. Look Martha implored Oh My God Oh Look Looky Look. They are running around the fire with their weenies up in the air stuck with sharp sticks. Martha seems embarrassed and implores Janice to conceal the thing, she chases Janice in a halfhearted attempt to suppress it. Her voice is low and growling. But Janice will have none of it, Oh my God look isn't it phantazdick! isn't it growtesk! isn't it! Look at its mouth oh my God Goddamn isn't it? You better watch your language Janice on this public beach. This slowed things down a bit. Let's just eat them Martha, OK? OK.

A Epic

He stood before the darkling plain.

The combination came before his eyes, his eyes located it. The Combination next entered his ear and knocked directly on the brain itself.

His brain went to the door and opened it and asked who's there?

The stranger said we are the Combination. Shelter us from the rain.

There's only one of you the brain observed, it takes 2 to make a combination.

Not where I come from, they answered.

Of Eastern Newfoundland, Its Inns & Outs

With a yellow soft edge the moon rose waning. It moved over them and they saw it after the passing of each squall. No more dust on the road. The weariness of car travel lay in their limbs, a peculiar kind of delicious exhaustion. So they laughed a little, and were slightly cynical about their destination. They looked at the map repeatedly even though there was but one road and they were on it. And the direction could only lie ahead, since the direction which lay behind was the direction from which they came. There were no side roads, no forks. The curves were long and visible. But the road had a way of increasing while its length was at any point known, like the universe with each new refinement of the instruments possesses a "new" largeness and is brighter than before suspected. There is a difference. This Road grows dimmer, their destiny goes toward the ultra small.

They have some candy bars. An opened package of cookies. The water in the canteen has gone largely to relieve the dryness created by the cookies. When the road moves down by the coast here and there for a few miles they have a chance to look out to sea at the fishing boats. They fly past rows of the stacks of drying salted fish and then quickly through the cluster of habitations these fishing people use to keep them from the mighty attack of the winter. And then they are up and away back of the cliffs, across a stretch of muskeg, by the side of a glacial scooped pool filled full of bright brown liquid filtered through the gardens of peet. The air in the nostrils comes like raw iron from the bogs.

These are not tourists. Nor are they casual travelers. They are not anything you might label in such a way as to design the condition of their being they. They are people returning thru a land of unincorporated citizens. There are no places to stop to *do* anything. They stopped arbitrarily once to enquire, for what? A place to stay. But there was still a little sunlight left of them and anyway, they knew there would be no rooms for them. Their car stopped nonetheless, backed up and turned in toward the beach then turned again between the shacks. When they stopped a little boy appeared at the edge of the woodpile and then a score of children around the corners of the dwellings. A handful of adult members of the community came along too, but in the distance from across the main road came a man who was a special person there because he came by himself. The driver told the occupants of the car he would see what was happening and got out. The spectators now numbered thirty or forty, everyone it seemed, who had nothing to keep them away at that hour. They wore masks made of a stiff attention to strenuous gales. Their eyes were lit from a deep space within them, small flames protected only by the deepness of their organized isolation. The driver spoke to them, to the orchestra assembled before him like they were one thing. You might as well know what he said as long as you keep in mind that what he said was more a matter of an exotic wavelength caught by the dish of a radio screen than any simple address.

Is there anyplace around here we might stay he said. Was it obvious to them that, put that way, anyplace was where they, or anybody else, might stay. Or did they understand *stay*. For the night, he said. Is there some place. Did he mean one of their shacks. He didn't say shacks. He said place. Any place. One of the problems was that none of the houses had a sign.

No sign. There was no way to even guess what these citizens might do, there was no sign on anything. For what they would not do they didn't need a sign. Can you tell me how far the next place where I can find a place to stay is. He immediately thought the way he had put that was a little complicated. He ran through his head the other combinations that question could be put in. In other words, I'm a show he thought. These people will stand here for all the combinations I got. He looked into the eyes of the man from across the road expecting to be dismissed at least by the voice this community might use to address the outside. The man was dressed for rain. He had his hands in his pockets and although he occupied the center of the dish he showed no inclination to speak. Perhaps he is simply the chief spectator and when I look at him I am looking into the medicine of this assemblage. He tried again. There are no rooms?

They tracked him. They studied the car. The color was a faded anachrome, the inmates looked out from the windows. This was one of their number standing before them who told them they had no rooms. This elegant passerby who spoke so easily and understood situations so clearly had just guessed the most obvious thing in this part of the world. He looked like a strange rock brought from the shore of another place. If he stayed around long enough they might set him on a shelf. But why is he asking. What does he want. He isn't drowning offshore, he is not weak from hunger. He must have got here on the boat. And the car too.

The wood smoke from the shacks mingles with the gusts of rain in the falling day. These people must have something to do, something to eat, some place to be inside. A perfectly normal night is coming. He smiled, not knowing who to thank, he thanked all of them since that had been their one insistent silence, that they were one. He got back into the car shaking his head saying well, I guess, I mean I'm pretty certain there isn't a place to stay here for the night. But then we don't want to stay here anyway. Let's see. What *did* I stop for. Oh yea, to find out how far it is to the ferry. I doubt if any of those people have been that far, anyway I forgot to ask. The arc of the community stood by. He thought of getting out again and they watched him think of getting out again but they could not imagine why he might do so. Perhaps he had thought of another question. Some other test of their intelligence. Like, how far it is straight up? That was the kind of question this community might go for, something to throw them off. Not like, they didn't have any rooms. They didn't have any food, they didn't have any brains, or they didn't have any lives is what all that must mean. The children were the first to move. This affair hadn't been exciting to them. They had a few other places they could go and they went. The older members of the community broke up more hesitantly and in fact they were not quite going to leave until the car left.

A delicate psychological equilibrium became evident as each party suggested to itself that its autonomy had been restored. The arc of the community balanced on its hips with the satisfied sense that another intrusion had been faced down. And furthermore, that the quality of the intrusion was so low-grade the community had not been called on to bat an eye, much less answer the so called question. The relief from inside the automobile was proportionate to the fact of that mechanical creature's exit. The assumption from inside was immense. Yet this is the law: In a confrontation of two parties the departure of one activates a deep sense of victory in both. This can happen simply because they are no longer in touch and therefore can't, in the crucial sense, monitor each others response. This nice structure, had the car's motor failed, would have collapsed in a heap too confused to describe. But the motor did not, thus the occasion was a rather pure instance of mutual self-satisfaction. As the villagers dispersed toward their suppers to digest with each enzyme of their hungry attention the isolation of and victory over the enemy the exchange inside the vehicle maintained the balance.

What we have here, the driver was saying, is an instance of north-south orientation, I mean these people have been on this limited axis so long they have literally, even if they remain figurative, forgotten what simple courtesy is. What's simple about courtesy, a member from the back seat asks. Yea. You said it. There's nothing simple about courtesy. In fact that's a kind of a late manifestation isn't it, no — what I mean is these people got cannibalism written all over them. It would have been very risky to stay there even if they didn't have any rooms, which is the curious way I put it. Maybe in fact that's what that stop means, I had to stop just to tell them something. Is that why you stopped, everybody was wondering. I think so. There's no *people* here even though there apparently are people here, like we see them along side the road. But their encampments are like sham. The occupation is obviously fish, but they don't seem to eat any, remember that cafe we stopped at they had nothing but campbell's soup. And have you checked out their kitchen middens are somewhat enormous pyramids of empty pork and bean cans. Are you sure they're empty? Well no. But that's the point. It might be worthwhile to go thru their cans. And what would it mean if they weren't, say, empty? All of them? Of course not, some of them have their lids hanging open, you can see that. OK, if there were some percentage less than 100 unopened that would mean, if you made a count, you could determine the factor of boredom. How would you arrive at that result? That's simple arithmetic, you'd divide the empties by the fulls.

Well, it's easy enough to say we don't want to stop here. But what did you mean, uh, when you said cannibalism, I don't think I noticed anyone with a T-shirt like that. Uh, I see what you mean — it's not like that. These people are straight out of the mesolithic but they were born last year. They haven't got any room of course because they haven't got anything they couldn't *move* altho they consider themselves firmly established no doubt. But all those pork and bean cans reveal a basic uneasyness deep in their own minds if you see what I mean. *Somewhere* down there they're recalling the time when they had to get everything together just to announce they were gonna wake up. You forget, all we have to do is snap our fingers, and the sun comes on. It wasn't always that way baby. Less than ten thousand years ago these types were trying to get used to the heat. And you could walk all the way across from the mainland. That's right, you got the picture. They didn't know whether to pick berries or make fish hooks. That's what's called a decision involving basic industry.

But how do you account for the fact that these people don't even eat their own fish, apparently they send the whole catch to somebody south of here. You see, the driver's companion continued, I'm not purely convinced these citizens aren't simple conscripts sent here to harvest this part of it, and when they've served their time they're brought home if they're still alive.

I thought you said Eat their own Flesh. But either way I don't see that as any difference. Time is determined by behavior, there's no time outside anyone's action in it. If someone sends you what's that but a variation of your sending yourself. It's just a post-glacial condition of the people on stage now, or what do you call modern man. The *point* is somewhere else — a north-south axis is that kind of set-up, it's an environment with a double orientation. This group of members comes struggling in with the very last specimen of the Great Irish Deer and everybody else is holding Wild Pig. Antlers spanned eleven feet. Well look it takes some rich vegetation to support fauna of that weight. What do you mean? Because if you got a pig you won't starve.

That certainly depends on what you have in mind for starve. A pig can root around and always find something. So if you live by eating the pig, who's living? *Pork and beans,* and don't mistake it, that's what's there right now. It's the north-south dilemma, from Spain to Finnmark, from Calcutta to Kalamazoo. The only problem that's come up so far is What to eat. And altho that takes various forms it's still the only problem. And that's the whole thing? That's right, that's it, because it includes everything, for example what to wear, where to go, which is simply the elimination of where not to go, what not to see, what the opposite might be and so on. You're looking, in other words, right at it. The mesolithic comes in unchanged. Pure quandary. What do you do when the Ice Melts, the Sea Advances, the Animals Shrink, The Trees Grow and the Grass Dies et cetera. Pork, and, Beans. In that order.

Satisfied that the departure had been defined they drove on in silence for a stretch of fifteen miles of curves across the tundra and along the segments of beach road where they again encountered encampments one much like the last. Oh, you mean Agriculture, someone said. And the difference that made. The driver started to turn his head then swerved away from an oncoming pickup truck, That's the backscatter, he said. And that makes them cannibals? That's right. Since they are the result of pork and beans, that must be what they are, so if they eat pork and beans, you see what I mean. That's a simple way to summarize 9 or 10 thousand years, don't you think? Yes it is, but really it's more like 7 or 8. And you have to keep in mind that the last people to have to deal with a major change are the most desperate. They are often called irrelevant by the later types who know what they want. So what about canned watermellon? You said it, but they want it.

The whole assembly was now keeping a close watch for the turn toward the ferry landing. No one knew the name of the town but they knew it was not Harper's ferry. In the North someone had said that one house at this landing had rooms for which there were no occupants and it was of these rooms they were to enquire. There was the name of a lady. At a filling station the driver got out and gave the name to the attendant and was given instructions. The others could see him looking in the direction they would go, they watched him through the rhythm of the wipers standing with his neck drawn in the rain.

They drove down a road to the water, they could see the landing and the strip of water illuminated by the moon. The boat was tied up, a low yellow light came from the engine room. They turned right just before the landing. An arm of the bay came in so that the house stood by the landing on the south shore.

The kitchen when they entered was unaccountably warm. The atmosphere was steamy and hot like midnight in the jungle. The lady of the house stood by her electric range smiling an exotic smile which seemed some disturbing result of hybridization, nothing evolved. She was perhaps 1.50 m. tall, her husband, who stood in the archway leading to the other rooms was a few cms. taller. Someone had made the arrangements so that when the group got itself all the way into the room there was nothing much to say. They stumbled around for a while and then got headed into the next room and up a short flight of steps to a hall which gave on to the rooms.

These were rooms. There were two, side by side as if they were in a larger structure. This part of the house lay by the water. Long delicate mosquitoes swung around the light bulbs in both rooms. They came down past the eye on their vicious trips. Howard in his room was trying to save his wife and children from the mosquitoes and in so doing stood on the bed with a newspaper with which he stopped them against the ceiling. The children were crying irritating the uncirculated air of the room. Next door the driver lifted the covers of the bed to check out the mattress and then wandered around the room reading the small frame pictures whose messages left the mind blank with stunning domestic messages like don't forget to empty the garbage lest you forget. And, a bright rosy sun rose one morning in front of a pale blue sky. One of the frames held him in a spell before it, this one was printed in hypothetical handwriting:

> SHE who gives
> Birth to a doll
> Will lose will
> And grow mad

The driver called his companion who sat on the bed staring up at the ceiling, tell me what you make of this one he said, it's the heaviest yet — and check that picture it's printed on, so faint you can't hardly see it, you see what she's doing, she's under an umbrella and She's got a box under her arm, the round box is under her arm and something is pouring out of it. That's right she's on her way home, she'd gone to the store or something for her mother and now she's taking it home. Your reading is completely correct. See the smile on her face, she's in her head, completely, losing all the salt. Will her mother be angry the driver's companion asked. Well I don't know, I've never thought about that but I'd say she'll have to straighten out and go right back for more. Stoned? I think there's no doubt about that. You've never seen that picture before, of course. Oh sure, it's been around a long time — it must be one of the dreamiest packages ever devised.

Oh, the message I can't even get to. But I agree with you, it's not the same spasm as God Bless Our Home. And technically it is an expression of selfconfidence — hey did you hear that? the biggest crash I ever heard and the lights are out. Open the door. They're all out. Don't move, stay here, there's not even an eerie glow, look here comes a candle.

That was quick! Howard's face was jambed up to hold back several megatons of laughter — Man I just broke the bulb in our room trying to stop the mosquitoes, I don't know what to do — do you hear the patter of little feet? They're all over the place. I think it's those dolls, did you see how they were lined up on the sofas when we came through the living room? Did I see them, there must be thirty of those creatures in this place, how do you think they got here? They could have taken the ferry or they might have come in by car ahead of us. But they got some cold shit going. You think they got something to do with this strange smell. I don't know. I *don know*. This place is fused now, there's no doubt about that.

C. B. & Q.

IN THE EARLY MORNING the sun whipped against the plate glass of Tiny's restaurant, reflecting the opposite side of the narrow dusty street where the printer's shop, the saloon, another restaurant waved in the quiet morning, in the distorted glass. This was Tiny's place. He was called Tiny for the usual reason. About 6:30 every morning the place was full of construction workers, and an occasional rancher who had been stranded in town the night before. At night, in front, until 8:00, were several railroad section men, with the exception of Sunday night, talking about Denver or Kansas City, or talking in cruel tones about John C. Blain the concessionaire who handled all the meals for the Burlington railroad. But most of the section men, the gandies, stayed close to their bunk cars, in a park of rough square shape and next to the tall thin grain elevator that could be seen for several miles coming from the east, from Belle Fourche, or from the west.

Back of the restaurant the half desert began. Immediately. There was a banged up incinerator fifty feet out, in the desert of short pieces of barbed wire and rusted tins. Beyond wasn't a desert exactly. Sheep, and probably some cattle, grazed there, over on and on past the layers of soft hills. A map shows the open range to extend far into Montana.

On past Tiny's restaurant, past the hardware store and a vacant lot with an old ford grown in the rear of it, was the New Morecroft Hotel. Buck stayed there. He had new scars right under his lower lip and over farther down on his left jaw after he had washed with strong hotel soap, more bright scars stood red and looked quite becoming. He had been three days so far without paying so that Simms the thin owner shifted his feet on the linoleum floor when Buck returned to his room in the evening. Outside the low ceilinged lobby, on the front porch, it was quitting time for the construction workers and they hung around while their foreman took the days' count of everyone's hours into the small office thrown up with new rough lumber next to the hotel. It was the last building in the block and beyond it was a vacant lot and beyond that were the bunk cars of the gandy crews on a siding leading off to the grain elevator. To the left across the road, the gandy crews stood in bunches or stretched out resting on the lawn. The length of the dirt street was in shade by 5:15.

Soon after, the rain fell slowly into the street and raised quick pockets of dust. Simms lifted his sharp elbow from the glass show counter where he kept odds and ends, a 1952 calendar, a mail-order catalogue, a dusty carton of aspirins, and moved to the front window where he propped a foot on the ledge and stared with his cheek on his hand at the increasing wind in the poplars outside and the rain that was now hard. The park was empty and the rain drove the small border of willow trees toward the ground. Buck came to the window all washed up and said that them gandies could sure move when they wanted to.

Outside town, off the highway to Gillette, about four miles to the right was a considerable mound of gravel. Except for a layer of sandy dirt a foot or so thick on the top, the gravel below was of a varying grade. A fleet of ford dump trucks were lined up near the contractor's shanty and the rain spread roots of light yellow clay over the hoods and down from the cabin tops onto the windshields. The yellow caterpillar sitting in the mouth of the pit threw stream jets up from its hot radiator and from the tin can covering its vertical exhaust pipe. Reed, the contractor, was frying some eggs for his supper, and he sometimes glanced out his window to the river curving around the base of the gravel hill where two of his workers, from

South Dakota, had a trailer hidden in the willows. The smoke from their camp stove stayed close to the ground this evening. This was almost the end of the contract. The gravel stockpile out by the highway across the rolling range was lengthening day by day and the regular peaks made by the dumps were growing dark and shining in the rain. Virgil Reed would pass the stockpile as he turned onto the highway to town and see he would have to hire another driver if he wanted to finish the job before the end of June.

2

BUCK WOULD NOT go near the post office. And he always waited around for some time before he asked Simms if he had any mail that day. A letter from the gang at Papy's tavern in Wichita came yesterday but it only mentioned his wife and kid in Mississippi and nothing about the accident. When the car crashed at the red light intersection in Wichita Buck threw out of the car and was in K.C. the next morning. He got drunk that day and saw lots of old acquaintances who worked with him in Nebraska and others he didn't know but who knew those he did, from Denver to Omaha. It was hot that day in Daddy's tavern in Kansas City. The three piece band smiled as they sat sweating on the little band box between the two toilet doors. The heavily built man with the curly hair stood on his crutches by Buck's stool and bent his neck to hear the talk about the guitar and drum. Max was one half Cherokee and Buck thought he had known Max. Max was sure. And when Buck found out Max had nine dollars and a ride to Wyoming on the Burlington that afternoon at 4:00 he went across the street to the gandy hiring hall and hired in too. When he got back to Daddy's Max was in with a tiny old woman who had already got three dollars away from Max. Buck sat brooding in the booth under the band box and once in a while glared at Max. He snapped hard language across to the bar and asked Max if he was indian. Max weaved slowly and smiled at the little woman who pulled on his flannel shirt. He smiled into the crowd and said he was indian from way back and old Buck was going with him anytime now to Wyoming. At the last minute Buck jerked away from old Sheila and had a cab on the curb outside Daddy's.

Max sat upright and stared all night, across

the aisle from Buck, out the window. The train drove through the darkness up the Kansas line to Nebraska. In the station at Kansas City they had only given their names to the man at the gate with a list. In the car there were no white tabs on the windowshades by their seats. They rode free to the job in Wyoming. At Grand Island, Nebraska Max got off the train and went into a restaurant back of the depot. He thought he might go back to Daddy's. Sheila was there every day he bet. Since coming from Illinois with the man who took dogs to a hospital there, he hadn't been with a woman. In the still waiting car Buck opened his eyes. He blinked when he felt his swollen lips were tighter this morning than they had been since the accident. He licked them and wandered through the car and down to the platform to look for Max. Max must have five dollars left, unless he buys too much to eat. Buck found him in the restaurant with some of the other travelers to Wyoming. Buck ordered a cup of coffee and said to Max that they might not have to gandy if there was other work there, maybe on a ranch or road work. Max thought if he didn't like the setup, the look of things when they got there he might shove on to Oregon, he had an uncle who was a foreman in a mill in Klamuth. They came back through the depot just as the train moved off toward the border.

It was unusual to arrive on Friday afternoon because there was no work Saturday or Sunday. Buck swung up into the dining car and took the last seat for dinner, away from Max who was avoiding his eyes now that he had determined to go back to Daddy's to drink beer with old Sheila. And late in the evening Max blinded the first passenger back east. It was on Monday morning that Buck decided he wouldn't work on the section. He ate their cold fried potatoes for two days.

3

VIRGIL REED CAME ALONG the pavement into town, through the increasing waves of rain, between the ditches on either side and broken weeds and long grass that had been earlier in the spring burned by the hot winds pouring in from the south-east. He had shaved after finishing his supper and there were still wet nicks on his neck below his chin and he dabbed them with his handkerchief from time to time. He knew that his new catskinner was a man that would work, he knew how to push the gravel. With Boyd the matter was simple: if you are a small man, you have to use your hands and feet to move. All day on the dusty cat he had crammed the accelerator to the floor and ground into the earth, with his visor cap pulled down tight on his forehead he had ground the blade into the earth, let it up and down quickly and infuriated the truck drivers by spilling over onto their road under the gravel loader. With the engine roaring all around the small hills that surrounded the pit, the shattering engine in command of all the air and Boyd was in command of the engine, back and forth across the opening to the pit he pressed the large, dirty, yellow caterpillar and acknowledged no one's presence until the end of the day, when soon after the rain started on the hot metal covering the engine, he told Reed about the defective left brake. Reed said he would see to it.

Now Reed rounded the corner into town, past the tight groups of willows, past the deserted filling station, went the length of the street and stopped in front of the New Morecroft Hotel. Through the glass he could see Buck standing with Simms. Buck suddenly faced Simms with his hands out of his pockets and nodding several times said some words and turned to go. Out on the porch Reed met him and they started back down the street towards Pages' saloon.

In Pages' Boyd was at the bar. It was nearly dark outside. The rain along the muddy street had slackened to a fine quiet regularity. The rain was quieter throughout the whole town. Up on the hill outside town on the highway to the east, in the filling-station-grocery store where Buck was running up a small grocery bill, and saving credit stamps against a large red ornamental lamp with a white meandering shade for his mama, and beyond that, was a small opening in the grainy clouds, weak light from the sun as it went down in the north-west in back of the hill.

In the bar Boyd sat by himself away from the general noise centering in the last booth on the wall opposite the bar toward the back of the saloon. Some road construction workers heavily persuaded each other that the wage was bigger in North Dakota or at the white horse dam job in Montana and that you could work endless hours but it was dangerous. The big fellow with the wrinkled forehead had skinned a cat on a high bluff where the push was so inclined that you had to be quick to save the rig and yourself from going over at the last minute. Boyd listened to their tales and jerked his head as he finished his beer and looked their way with his short curled smile. Through the room of noise he shouted to the heavy-stomached man with the wrinkled forehead that he could drive any earth mover made, and that he didn't need to think that since he was such a big bastard he could talk so smart. But Curly didn't hear him then because one of the others in the booth had started to tell of a job the summer before near Butte.

Buck and Reed came through the door and took stools next to Boyd. Boyd relayed their orders down the varnished bar to the bartender, and Reed went on about the job out at the pit, how he was thinking of moving his equipment to Cheyenne as soon as this county job was done.

Through the open door Buck could see several men he recognised from some other summers and he thought again of how he could get his mail without a direct address. They were sure to be on his trail. Boyd asked Reed if the job down at Cheyenne would be a big one and Reed didn't answer so Boyd turned his head away from Reed and Buck and looked at the group in the rear booth where there was now an argument between the large frowning man with wrinkles in his forehead and another road worker, thinner and tall, who said he could cut as fine a grade with a scraper and cat as the big frowner could with a patrol grader. The frowning man's answer to this was to take his opponent by the khaki shirt and lift him quickly on top of the table spilling several glasses of beer. The noise was overflowing, even out on the street the knots of workers knew. Back of the bar under the long slender tubes of green vapor two hula-girl lamps wiggled their rubber bottoms and the bartender was debating his duty. Boyd slid off his stool and took it with him as he made across the floor to the battle. He had cracked it on the large man's back twice before it was thrust back into his middle at the end of the third swing.

Outside on the bumper of the car with his face bleeding Boyd wiped his small hands on his pants' legs smearing the blood in long stripes and crying. He sobbed in jerks as he tried to clean out between his sticky fingers. He told Buck that he always wanted to be a mason anyway, that that was a real trade, you didn't have to worry about jobs and the right kind of money once you made it. But they wouldn't let him train for it when he got out and there were always so many on the waiting list for apprentice that he couldn't see it. Buck said he had a good job down in Wichita but the goddam foreman had it in for him because he broke three springs on the truck in one day on that bad road and he got fired. Boyd had calmed down and said he had intended to go south for the winter, maybe to Tucson or Albuquerque but he was sure as hell going to be south when the winter hit this place. And he didn't see what Buck saw in Wichita. He could go anywhere anyway because he had a car that the back seat came out of and could be used to sleep in he said.

The Terrifik Refinery in Biafra

Marvelous Refinery is not my name. My name is Gregory "Jim" StoptKlok. And whoever named me knew something about my condition. Really knew it; so if Terrifik Refinery is a disease; and he is a disease like you can't stop white corpuscles and that makes the disease large, something you can *see,* an idea, the size of an insect, then I'm a whitethroat still in that hope, the white hope, which means simply nothing actually! To be BRight! in other words that's nothing except a quality not equality over and over again. That's all and if you can't make that you're not, Nothing. If you're not white you don't *have* to be bright; you disappear into the invisible, into all the ad-vantages. White can always be seen trying to prove it and that appendage is clumsy — you'll think about yourself if you be white; everytime. Sometimes I *think* I'm White Indian Wild Cinnamon. A mystique from the dictionary.

I live in this rat-trap town on the plains. Everytime I go out to my car there's this foreign car parked ahead of me, a V.W. or a Volvo Wagon, and on the rear bumper there's a sticker. Help

Save Biafra, which is a paperdrive. They get it all together at the county Court House; tear up tons of old news and send it back as confetti — ! the discussion is exported home very much cut up. One word at a time can take a lot of time. But back here there's a lot of surplus time — it may not start, or stop, but it's cheap, Unless, you try to send it to Biafra. And *that's* why it's stuck on the bumper.

So I get into my car and sit there getting it warm and that sticker has my mind. I'm bright like that and you see I *think* what a poor sad-assed bumper that man's got — a whole statement sittin there to be pushed by any myopic driver who turns the corner and if it said Help Push Biafra — but they're not gonna feel that either. This owner ahead of me is a stamp licker and yard raker so he takes how things go and look, seriously! He's banked on someone looking at it that way, that's it, all the way down this mountain, into these streets there is a shitslide. The man comes along, slaps some of it on his bumper and drives off to the sick ward. It's got something to do with why I can't say no to a construct like Terrifik Refinery. He's something like Biafra in this sense: He's been made. And in this sense: He's been destroyed with Help. Also in this: When he's dead the sticker will be changed. He's about 40 which is older than Biafra, but he'd never get that point, instead he thinks that number of years is special and is going to get him some free attention like his beard. And he's Alcoholic. An internal combustion engine. Of course there is a certain minimal difference between a Distillery and a Refinery, they are practically interchangeable. But internal combustion is something simple and anyone who overtakes you with that problem *is going to make your whole existence stink!*

Get the fuck off that set as soon as possible, make your own exit, if necessary right through the wall. Don't do anything *un*necessary! Anyway, so I'm bright and I know exactly what's happening when Terrifik Refinery says to me Stopt you're the *only* one who understands me — you're the only one who knows how to help — I've got no friends and *I know I'm important*. What? I'm important! Oh, well sure. Like the Eiffel Tower. Where have I heard that. How is he important? he *says* it. That's good enough I seem to remember from what I've been told but What I ask myself is wrong with another Idea — this Fuck is not only *not* important but over that he's drunk; which means he stinks and is not important in a very *recognizable* way. And making a hit off me with some

News he got somewhere about if he *exists* he's important which might have come from a Nation of Hard Drinkers over the ocean. All this goes on at home. Built on some land, some site, at the edge — no matter how small you make it those specimens will invariably crawl to the edge. Important. They *want* to look like they're falling over. They think that's what's gonna make them look important. A standard stall — *quit,* then call everybody back for another start.

And that's it — look at him in their interiors. He'll claim that as a possession and then say that's the hang up! — !the interior — He bought this house on the edge, Nice House, and — that's its true name. Once you have what you want you can blame it. There are some Nice trees in back "that go with it". Talk to the trees. They have another story. They say they walked up one night and stood there watching him through the window and couldn't move the next morning. They were *studs.* Thats the truth! — ! there's no way for them to get off that land now; they'll have to stand there and take it. His shit about owning them.

And, he claims he owns me. He makes that claim real by using a device he didn't even invent and doesn't even have to know how to run. He says to me he's important, and because I'm

StoptKlok and can say that's shit, you're NOT important, or, I don't even want to use your filthy word, opposite words confront each other across the canyon. He's got me, the notice is in the prince Albert can. Tacked to the tree in plain sight. He says all men have it. But the notice inside the can makes it read *only him*. And he'll beg you with some kind of flattery to understand how much he appreciates your understanding his problem. And if you say its *nothing!* and besides you can't quite make all he's saying because he's so Drunk he can't move words past the swill in his mouth he mumbles oh sure; you're the only one around here I can talk to, StoptKlok, I don't *have* any friends. Do you know what that means? I'm alone, I'm square, nobody's gonna come over to see me! So *I* say how can you be important, Terrific, if you're square? that sounds like you've got lots of company, all of it unimportant. Why don't you find something to do with the rest of your time? For instance even in a town like this which crawled to the edge and died you can invent an occupation which will make you distinct in at least your own eyes and if you're important already you might focus that identification a little, forget that woman and child you ran down last week, you knew the judge socially, you know your minister more than that. *And* you can fire him any time policy looks to be active. Just run it on the spool backwards and make it the same program the other way — for instance, *stop drinking,* and don't drive a car; and get up out of the grave, nobody's going to notice. And start walking the other way, if anybody asks questions tell them you didn't see yourself and then call your lawyer, that whole race came into being in order to handle the claims against your safety.

That's good advice. But *I'm afraid I'll commit suicide.* Well I'm afraid you won't. What? I said I'm a parade of such ideas. Does your wife know you're out. Oh! oh her. oh! my wife oh she's alright, she's *very* understanding. I'm, uh half my trouble comes from how good she is. Jesus; I'm glad she's not bad: What? I said some wives profit from their husbands mistakes. Or look at it this way, you bought a policy for the "family" and they can live inside it for 68 years so in a sense you can afford another form. What? Well that could be almost anything, but the way it's going you're using your form like it was a bucket. What? I mean you haven't got it into the correct form — if for example somebody dumps all the ingredients for an oatmeal cookie into your hand you can eat it but that

43

doesn't mean you got what you asked for, necessarily. What? An oatmeal cookie.

Oh! Look! This has been a tradition for *so* many years. This has been a springboard for so many boys that you can hardly get rid of it. The American People want it to be there. You're doing just fine. Just remember if you can't drink don't drive *and* if you can't drive don't drink because in the latter case you'll really be stranded. I'll take you home now and maybe we can work something out next week.

It was one of those warm days we sometimes get in late February and it was Sunday so we drove straight across the campus onto the west edge. Inside the Nice House Terrifik Refinery asked if I'd like a drink and I said Bourbon straight 2 ice cubes. Oh you can have a drink he said, it won't bother me, I won't drink. Good I said, I *need* a drink. I'm desperate, you're terrific.

So you've been attending the meeting of Alcoholics Anonymous? do you ever talk about what's on what's left of your brain. Oh. uh, no! no I never speak. Those people are real people though, no intellectuals, but people who've been through a lot, they know about life. What's that, in their case? huh? What. I say you've got yourself a drink. Yea, well I feel I have to have it, that's the only way I can live with it. Do you feel there's any connection between this present difficulty you're having and the navy? The marine corps. Ok, the same thing from this room. What do you say? Why don't you talk at AA? Oh no, I just couldn't do that. What do you do, sit there enjoying somebody else's confession? you must be like a volunteer spectator at a torture, like the use you make of a car only less active? Uh would you like another. Yea! I *need two,* I'll never survive the liquor condition without liquor. Its appeal is obvious: in a nasty situation anyone might be attracted to the cowardice in himself: *Lets have a drink* is the epitaph to a whole category of reality called Lunch. You want a Drink? No!

Gloria returned from work. Doors click and shut. She arrives at the fireplace behind a smile obtained from a paraphrase of textbooks on the psychology of Bell Telephone. Her pleased attitude is a story in which these two boys have been "drinking" and eventually they end up back at the house, boys always come home. Finally, it's always time to go back, to see somebody you really know, let them be with you at that hour, smiling through the details of a day that was like the one before it, even though the sun won't agree by a minute and a half.

Hello Gloria. She's using what she thinks is a secret look at the Refinery. More help on the way. The tankers can be seen off shore, waiting to come through the gate in the seawall. Oh! oh sure Everybody has been *so* understanding. Wait a minute, there are others besides me? What? oh! the head of the Engineering department. That's interesting, I'll bet he builds cool bridges, an expert in refrigeration. The head of the Engineering department. He says this with renewed determination. Is very *Understanding*. Look! I'm forty — do you know what that means. Lets see. I tried hard to think. Couldn't come up with *any* guess given only one clue. Well, it means I'm forty. Years old? Yea! But the point is, I thought we agreed, your Important. Yea! his head wandered. Look I said, desperate again and made realistic by the liquor, this liquor is really putting my head down, But it suddenly occurs to me you might beat the whole thing. *Change your name.* At forty. Sure, good time, you've used it long enough. Quite a few people do that these days — take up Islam and change everything — there's a great deal in a name — new home, new wife, new town, new car, Gold Rush, what about it? I'm going to quit my job. Good! That's probably the place to start — takes up too much of your time, you'll be able to devote *all* your attention to yourself; after you've found it. Oh you've got some good advice Jim. I know it. They don't call me "Jim" for nothing.

But. Oh I'm beginning to lose it again. Goddammit I *know* I'm important. Sure you are. I don't wanta do anything intellectual right now and besides I'm episcopalian. And I'm 40. Yea, inches around the waist. What? You've got no time to waste. Oh; *Time*. Yea that's what I want. Want? Want! What do you want. I just —

He threw his hands out and the trees stared through the windows, waiting to learn something more about the man who owned them —

WANT. Just Want! That's all. See. I JUST WANT! I just WANT. Gloria had by now changed into her home smile. A smile pleased with the trees' attendance, and comfortably familiar with the insatiable mouth of the fireplace and her mouth shared the asthetic triviality of that orifice which stood there by us through thick and thin in the forced air. *She'd* never feed the trees to the fireplace. They knew that. Gloria is good and wood is got from a woodcutter. A nasty business. But they obviously were not so sure of him. Ex-marine. So they waited to learn *what* he wanted. I knew that was going to be difficult — what does a golfer want who drives the ball? To reduce his strokes? A hole? I decided to help them.

My first question was what did the trees expect, bending toward the window, in the wind. None of them were very old. Ten, fifteen years at most. Skinny, badly nourished on poor fill in one of the early bulldozings toward the edge of this town, itself on the edge of the plains. In the branches of one of the most forward trees sat a cardinal, singing his own number. How did he get his own number? How will Terrifik get his own number? I reminded myself to try the trees and stopped listening to the answer of the bird. I began, have you noticed the sun is rising and the time is 6 P.M.? Where? uh, oh, sun. The trees turn to look, and turned back, more interested in the glass side of the box under them into which the rays cut. What does he want. He said it. Want. *That's* meant for me, the trees will never be included. They always hand you the solution and make you figure out what went into it. You must start at the end of the story and work back. The scholarship of Boredom. *What do you want!* asked Gloria, Bourbon or Quit. Quit? Oh that's a new soft drink, "Quit, the soft drink that doesn't put you on," dietetic, you might not dig it, it's not as good as cream soda, you know that drink? I

do, sure, my favourite, it really does put you on.
Well which. Cream Soda. I don't have any unless I run to the store. Don't do that! Quit!
Well I was going to anyway. Now? Sometime!
There's no time like right now! I suppose you're right. What will we do with him? Gloria's phantasy led her away but no one knew where she was. Her smile stayed at home, turned automatically toward the door as the children returned from the neighbours.

They all passed by like tourists. So Quit? So Quit does it Gloria. You can't mean that! I don't mean anything but you ought to understand something basic about drunks. Her smile went into the bedroom. What's that? she called back. Their perception is exactly like the grain from whence their poison comes, ten thousand acres of it swaying in the gravitational wind like the far travelling waves of the sea, *they're all ears*. Huh? 40 years, thats how old I am. I lived half my life! You'll be lucky. Huh! and lived is questionable. Would you like some more bourbon or whatabout Quit? I wanta go look at the trees! Fine, just turn your chair and talk to them, their reddiness has a brief history. But if you go out there you'll lose. What? Why! I mean whatyamean? The sun's rising and you're in no shape to meet it. Sun's not rising — that's out west! What time is it. Don't know, my clock is stopped. How come you knew the time? When. Oh sometime. When the kids came home. What kids? That was before the sun rose. Ah. So they're *your* kids? Certainly, how do you think they got here? Ah and those are your trees. Well certainly, how do you think they got here? That doesn't explain it. Your trees at least are going to leave, and soon. Yea, it must be spring. Where's gloria! That's one way to your problem. What? Religion. I'm episcopalian. Uh huh. That's sort of, Well isn't that more of an attitude than a religion. What do you mean? What do I mean? Ya! I thought you'd tell me you belong. Oh no. Oh no. It's a religion. YES its a religion. Gloria! Gloria! Once more. whGLORIA! they just opened the gate.

Gloria walked out of the hall into the room. She wore a house coat and above her smile was a towel in which she had her hair. Lighting a cigarette she asked, well what'll it be Bourbon or Quit "the drink that turns you on" I didn't hear it that way the first time or I think there's some pot around here someplace, her smile shifting slightly from home to downtown. Although, she added, I keep looking for the sign to the freeway. Just stay on this route and you'll find it. Sure! we'll find it Terrifik put in. Isn't he marvelous she observed. No, Terrifik, I said. Great! lets name him that. How will we spell it? I think with a K, like terrifik. Yes, that does give it a kind of respectability. Yea, it looks more like a name that way. And, Gregory, it sounds like a degree! Sure does. Her house coat turned to the window. Whats happening to the sun? It continues its distant labour. All that work. What do you mean? That's a terrifik question. Oh did he ask you that. Not lately. Maybe the sun will learn to stand still, we *lose* half of it this way. Maybe that's what upsets the trees. No I think thats the wind. It takes a strong wind to upset trees. Shall we let Terrifik sleep? Unless you can dream up something else to do with it. Anyway I think I'll go home. Gloria walked into the kitchen. Not going to the freeway after all? No, well that's what anybody does, and this hasn't been after nothing. Yea, she said from the door, I know what you mean. Great! Bye! Thanks!

Several days later the phone rang! Jim looked at his own number. It's a lousy poker hand, not even a pair. Is that possible with ten digits. He had to include the Area Code — he couldn't stand up under the weight of a purely local number. He tried to locate the missing number. Couldn't find it. Ah, a pair of nines! pure speed — the strongest single number. Ninety-nine. Pillage and Rapine. All the way around the trads! He picked up the phone, took off the handle. Hello! oh it's Terrifik. No, the voice fell off the wire, it's terrible. You're Terrifik. What? I mean if you've got a new name you're 1 week old. Think of that, you can already talk on the telephone. Well, at least you can pick up the handle. What did you say. I cant quite make it out — you've been *drinking?* Gloria understands! You flipped the car end over end. You kicked the squad car radio off its hanger when they took you in? Yea thats right thats destroying state property. It sure is. Any engineer could tell you that. So it was really fucked up huh, couldn't do its work. Silence! I'll bet. Dead band. Well uh what did the force think about that . . . they were . . . I can imagine. But they took you home and put you to bed. Very understanding. I'd say it's a good thing they're so understanding. If you get violent like that understanding is something you can use. You don't remember a thing. Well even that's helpful. That was later? When you got home? You *did* that? Bit the top off a Wine bottle because you couldn't find the corkscrew! Yea, I can believe it fucked your mouth up . . . So that's why you ended up in the hospital . . . terrifik . . . I say

— you've been active . . . oh? Pulled the needles and tape right off your arm and walked home in the rain. Terrifik. Thats more determination than I've heard about recently. So what happened when they came to pick you up again . . . and how did they solve that problem? it's a drag to drive without a steering wheel. Yea, well let's hope it's all over remember, don't drink, in your case it might help everyone. How's Gloria. She's gone, took all the kids, that's real comprehension. Oh that's desperate — you were finally released and on the way out you shot your hand thru a half inch plate glass door! Yea, they'll do that, ligaments jump like rubber when they're cut. Snapped right up your arm and all the way down your back! That makes it a problem to sit down. Thats what they meant when I called up and was told you had a broken arm. No. Not quite the same thing. Sounds more like your arm Disappeared. Say, before I forget it there's a little job I'd like to do on my telephone. Well I want to change the number. I don't like the hand I've been dealt — what's the number? wow! Have you got the right party. No, no, man this is not the 1st National Bank. No. No. I haven't got the weather and I haven't got the time.

Driving
Across the Prairie

My sister drove the car. The random news of the town was ordinary and dull with the civic vengeance of small places. I hadn't until this afternoon been back for 15 years, and true to the morbidity of the gossip I saw the people's faces slip by as their names were mentioned in marriage and death, illnesses prolonged or brief, the cripples and how they were getting about, the victims of stroke and the rate of their defection, the new houses, those torn down. What had been reported in a letter, what seen, what guessed, what could not or would not be imagined. And all this in the casual, equal tones of a report coming from some other part of the world. And my sister drove, cooly and surely because she is younger and already leaves all that concern slightly behind.

The outcome of old friends. The son of the dentist kept to the straight and narrow had gone like one of the principal victims of the fifties to the University of Illinois where he learned to drink without inhibition and is now a wholesale liquor salesman on the Coast. It was at the same great university I learned to mend a broken heart by practising on my own. But the accomplishment had been condemned as unuseful and I was failed as a scholar. The girlfriend who, because she could not bring herself to fuck in highschool, misunderstood life enough to give birth to a deformed baby after she was married to a certified public accountant and thought herself safe at last. There must be many such ironies lost inside the people of the town of my birth. And I don't mean that to have any sound but what it has. I am simply a letter-carrier in a time when the post office has become obsolete, thus all the news carried that way sounds ornate.

The town we lived in and knew to be green with trees and busy with men's work had contracted and the edges had acquired a scab of small houses. A glaring ring of the merely new. The river small and dirty, every willow along it removed. I have no claim in mind — that it is better or worse now — people work somewhere else and return at night to throw out the food from their tables. The barn wrecked, the house covered once more with an inferior siding of something fake and perhaps they *have* discovered that the durable is unendurable.

We drove the county roads and passed through Camargo. I had gone there one night to be handed a certificate which stated in an appropriately official way I had graduated from the 8th grade. All my friends, who looked exactly like me because they had red faces and their wrists stuck out and they were dressed like that for the first time, were prompted by several persons to think about what it meant, stand up, walk past, receive the rolled-up slips of paper tied with a string. No vibration at all remains of that Camargo evening, which simply means that I remember it rather than feel it. It was in a church that event took place and I notice as we move by that it, of course, has not changed. All those friends have dealt or been dealt, life. There is a different bridge over the river. One without overhead girders. Nothing to be seen. The engineering in this new thing has been concealed. There never was a connection with the universe here but that bridge was a beginning. And of cosmology these people were able to add nothing to what the red man left, of which they themselves assumed themselves to be unaware. But I notice an ironic contrary in the current practice, new since I've been gone, of sending rolls of toilet paper unrolling over the tops of trees, a practice which is accurately described by the linguistic humiliation Teepeeing. There is a most certain misunderstanding here of the nature of living things. Most all the subtitles one can find for Love prove to be unsatisfactory.

Buying a new television for my people was not the worst idea. Max picked it out, turned it on, ran it through its abilities and bargained with the paralysed dealer whose speech only he could fully comprehend. This transaction fittingly came at the end of the day. And when we got it home and plugged in the first thing shown on N.E.T. was a documentary called FAMINE in which a woman in India picked up single grains of wheat from a landscape as barren in that sense as the moon. Her body was quite near death but her eyes shone with a serenity difficult to believe from the inside of an american lower middle class house which has been robbed of life in a way death doesn't really cover. Educational Television one has no doubt can be marvelous, what it can show, what it can bring to the senses. If one looks closely there comes a knowledge rising back of the very people who Create it. The cosmetic eye of the sacred cow looks out from its 30,000 incarnations. The sounding of the temple bells in Illinois. And there seems to be no shortage of beef in this part of the country.

It is my place but not my time. Any place can be mine. Time is irrelevant. So the place is simply once again, now. Time after all, plants its seed in the place. With Television came a birthstone, which was not a stone, on a false metal chain in a plastic box which was offered entirely free of any reference to a birth date. Assorted, in a box. The birthstone bag. I might as well say here that the paralysed dealer was vulgar and vulgar precisely because of his paralysis. He went somehow with the vision, somehow sprang forth from the same inarticulation. There is no way to avoid seeing him the day the stones arrived in their box, pawing them with that physical discontinuity we have all come to praise in the name of small business.

Eddie I thought Johnson sent a lot of wheat over there to them people — but they say the rats ate most of it . . . it seems like they'd eat them dead people if they're starving so much. Why should I tell her. A baby, lying wrapped in a cloth on the plain. A man digging a hole to put it in with a piece of tin in his drought surrounded hands. So, like the son, I shall always make an attempt. I tried to point out that only Christians and certain other primitives eat the dead, and that the subject of this particular program was India. On the other hand of course they were no more free of error than other peoples. And stopped, just short of bringing the news that McNamara had spread, in any event, the word: either these people and people of like failing get with it or they shall be annihilated as a threat to a world which preaches the Future but puts its money on here and now. A dispatch from the world bank. Don't get excited. Whether you know it or not, you have already placed your bets. The locusts have been ordered.

My sister drove willingly and with a certain politeness based on an old respect she has for me. The trouble in her mind comes from the fact of my long hair and the red handkerchief I have around my wrist. An embarrassment I regret but can do nothing about. If I were to remove both there would remain the difference of my soul which cannot be cut by a simple barber. We drive slowly through the light snow of news in October, along the amish roads, around their black old testament buggies, the weight of their horsedrawn lives, the smiles, the waving. The rabbinist sense in which they dress themselves, and yet they arrange small stones in the shape of hearts and arrows, rock gardens with inset messages, a paganism they surely can't respect. I mean they don't have the time. We shall tolerate that as folk art. Their oddness is based on cash and is therefore no real inconvenience. They don't like the Dukaboars remove their clothes in public therefore their issues don't exist and their farms are neat. Their horses and buggies my sister says are a terrific hazard.

My sister has become middle class by worrying about public safety. The noneconomic path most people take into that subworld. I was never middleclass nor were my parents, I mean our safety was never public. Our poverty was public. As we sat in the car waiting to begin our journey through the country she tossed the package back to me. In it were what she called pep pills, a habit picked up from her doctor with whom she bowls on Friday night, pep pills which all the world knows fondly as speed. The american language still leans on the vocabulary of the girl scout. She knows better than that. And, of course, we know better than her. That's how it breaks down. Thinking to get the problem out in the open I remark that my hair is longer than hers. Silence. Raised eyebrows in the rear view mirror. That was not meant to be competitive nor was it taken that way, it was a challenge meant to give her the chance if she wanted it to explain why her hair is short, and to allow me then to add that it looks nice. My function as a letter carrier is to sort the mail so that when it is presented it will look interesting. The reference is to the alphabet of course not the post office.

I notice a certain hesitation which is new to my ears and I wonder about the source. Last night she guarded her speech and tried me with a mouth for the most daring of the presidential candidates. Again the question rises. When I agree with her she mistrusts it because she expects me to conform to what her notion of the educated response is. But she doesn't know that the response of the educated is simply a destructive impatience with the uneducated. No matter how you cut it we've got no time for them at all and whoever they elect will never be more than a matter of amusement for us. Line up all their pictures and we die laughing. Until they solve the paranoia of their bad choices. The new nervous worker's middle class. Which simply means that by definition they all agree with the dentist. I had to come to the interior to hear it. A girl I once thought I knew in a land I once thought I was born in. Perhaps that Milton imaginist is correct — it all happened another way. Is my mother too much my mother to be something else?

Thus on and on. There is no part of the consideration which can be taken away from the

central fact that I still love them though that
love increasingly requires the participation of
my own amazement. I made this discovery in
my recent attempt to leave Massachusetts: No
matter how the occasion demands a sober face
never dismount the superb form of your anima.
The facts of this warm October are black and
white here just as they were. Down the roads
between the brown corn which on the prairie
serves to eliminate the horizon. The semiper-
manent smudges of horror called employment
rise as surely as they are credit cards into the
air and the famously increasing population
reckons the time of the month and accepts any
indifferent birthstone from the cardboard box.
And I am not suggesting they do in fact have
a specific birth.

Her driving was cool and sensitive. She drives
the Olds low this afternoon, the only way she
could be a muse, at the wheel turning, turning,
when I whispered beneath the conversation.
Her aversion for the cemetery was natural. I
wanted to stand in front of the headstone of
my frenchcanadian grandfather and read it
again, William Ponton, 1875-1936, the only
reading material for my eyes in these few thous-
and square miles. My mother persisted in trying
to make me remember the death of someone

named Goad. I made a distinct and immediate pact with myself not to. The highschool across the road. My old school. Then we left, drove over to Old Town across the Embarrass, which is a tributary, to the Wabash. Past some places which are not there now because in our youth we burnt them down. Past the elevator where I once sold hot corn for 2.50 a bushel during the second war. Past the house of the richest girls in town, who had a pool table upstairs and went to a second rate but expensive girls school, and one of whom, I was reminded, had married a cripple. Then back. Across the river. Down main street. Four blocks of unchangeable stupidity I once thought indispensible to my Saturday nights. The vacant lot I suddenly realise was never vacant because there was never anything even vacant there.

So when I first saw him he filled the place like one of those resistant images no wear or weather or puncture of time can alter. He was leaning on the side of a car his head in the driver's window and his crutches in one hand. An aspect of red shot through my underconscious and the name Bobbie rose as the only remaining scrap of what he had once been to me. So here it was anyway, in him, my whole trouble with the place, nothing more or less than a vague dissatisfaction. Heavy. A strange fleshyness. Alert and possessed by the hesitating aggression of the born cripple. The irritating but necessary nerve to make his life possible. A reflection of the psychological principle of Illinois. Suddenly this face and body I knew more than my own out of all that was left. The durability is terrible, and the beauty is real, stripped of the environment I could have furnished him years ago. He comes forward through all my astonishment without it. Through the tension and the disgust, and my mother, who must have known the parents, and for all her attention to the morbid locus of the prairie was no help — try as she would all the cripples known to her. His smile as he saw us pass let me know there was nothing I could escape.

There is a moral law that the true end comes before the real end. We turned up a street and came around for another pass. The man had felt my brain at work on his identity thus his face glowed with absolute superiority and I acknowledged his triumph by turning away. And thought of other things. The girl with whom I could have made love had we not been products of war would not have had a deformed baby had we not thereby been crippled likewise, had we been free as the new time for which I want to make it very clear I thank God directly. We needed love. We couldn't have it. Everything we were made to understand was being proven elsewhere. I saved myself by letting my hair grow and establishing a ritual of my own person which even the lightest reflection will reveal as a dangerous thing to do. I sensed this afternoon what she had done and what my own relationship to it is. Because my sister had heard the story from the liquor salesman. I want to be able to look back into the faces of the old gods. That lineage, that result, that crippled stem of this country is made with the mind. There must be a way to stop it.

The Garden of Birth

His mother smoked Hashish. She was herself a garden and its outward expression was in the rich loam of the brown sense of her blue eyes ringed within a slightly black edging. Truly, it could be said that drug was her companion from the botanica. More than Grass. And she spoke of it as to an old acquaintance, and Grass she thought No thats close to a football game, in the end, you have to use your head, therefore it must be thick. Sometimes I miss Miss? I miss my sister. I miss my identical. When I turn around I miss her on the other side of me. Then I enter a state in which I find her. She is my There. I am her Here.

Sometimes when she turns to get into a more comfortable position he feels a new crowding in his bag and moves accordingly, an adjustment she could feel. Her sister could feel it. This is the way he formed the first notion of his mother's sister. He can begin to feel how the new people walk through the old world amazed, an amazone.

And in this period of his life, if you understand, along with the work that follows conception, turning into his nativity, he saw trees. She was sitting on the screen porch. A hot slowly undulating afternoon. A maroon tree and a yellowgreen tree moved the contacts together at the point where the tree would be. Later, in him, all trees would be.

And when she played the flute her heart beat would enter in the score and guide the playing with sometimes the accompaniment, his heart under hers. Learning to beat the source of relation. The still sway of treetops in the sidereal wind, a motion far slower than centuries.

So he had two trees in her eyes and his mother was his sister. And his mother as well as his mother's sister, could feel him outside her while he was in her, opening his hands in the precategorical fluid of his home.

The Sheriff of McTooth County, Kansas

It was a hot afternoon in July and Sheriff Ballmik lounged in front of the Rockchalk Cafe under the shade of a tin awning provided by the good lord. With him, leaning against the building, the heel of his boot hooked on his kneecap, was his Chief deputy, Jim McHead. Both men wore their hair shoulder length, Jim's was straight and black, and the Sheriff's was reddish and curly. The Sheriff wore a tee shirt across the dirty front of which was printed in red white and blue stars and stripes the title SHERIFF. The temperature under the tin awning at 3 p.m. was 105 degrees above zero. The time is shortly after that and the temperature a little higher.

Every now and then Sheriff Ballmik removed the Lucky from his mouth and stuck in a toothpick and walked back and forth in front of the cafe with his hands on his hips and a bottle of Schlitz stuck out of his back pocket. He smiled and slapped a citizen on the back and squinted into the blazing sun. Sheriff George Ballmik had begun the day the best way he could. At 7 a.m. he walked off the porch of his rooming house onto the sidewalk and there, lined up in a crack, was a blue cap.

That musta dropped right out of a spaceman's pocket, he said.

He threw it up in the air where it inscribed three quarters of a circle and fell dead center into his mouth and stopped far down in his neck. His adam's apple sent it on immediately.

Mescalin, the Sheriff said, and smiled.

Then he got in his car, turned on the siren, started the engine and drove down to his headquarters where he smoked a lot of grass and briefed his men on their Fourth of July assignments. The rest of the day he drank whiskey and beer. Yes, Sheriff Ballmik was in a good mood because he had started well.

The citizens of McTooth County had not had time to absorb the whole fact that George Ballmik had been elected yesterday. His candidacy was a welcome relief in a hot-spell that had spread out in front of the election like a prairie-grass fire. It made everyone feel cooler to have a joke to tell. He was unopposed as a Democrat in the primary, and furthermore it was reckoned there were not more than 12 or 13 Democrats in the county. Of that number he might get 4 or 5, but when it came right down to it the only vote he could count on for sure besides his own

was McHead's. His campaign had been waged on these few simple propositions —
1. Round up the drugs
2. Leave beer alone
3. Promote women
4. Fix the roads
5. Fresh air and
6. Make the county pay

all of which were ambiguous enough and so open ended they caused almost no end of discussion. The Republican proposals were too boring to list but they sounded suspiciously like they had been copied from the Sheriff's posters and the result was incumbent as well as challenger seemed to be saying the same thing. Nevertheless it was true that although George Ballmik was a colorful campaigner and the republican was drab no one thought for a minute of actually voting for a man who had as the symbols of his candidature a bronze-dipped 6-pack, a giant 8 foot Church-Key, and a constant companion who was so severely stoned he hadn't opened his eyes within anybody's recollection. But when the time came around none of this mattered.

What happened was not really very complicated. A printing error put Ballmik on the Republican ticket and the incumbent on the Democratic and there were no split tickets in McTooth County. The incumbent received two votes, presumably cast by Ballmik and McHead. Apparently the Democrats had not got their entire vote out. The incumbent had naturally refused to yield, whereupon he had been placed under arrest which he resisted. There was no other response for Deputy McHead. He drew with unbelievable slickness and blew out the incumbent's ten top teeth one at a time.

> Very neat job, the Sheriff said,
> That would have cost him some
> smash and a lot more pain to have the
> dentist do it, *now* get the mother-
> fucker out of here before I
> stomp his ass besides.

The interest in this event was created mostly by the news that McHead had waked up.

Although Ballmik had never once mentioned either law or order during the campaign it now became clear to everyone in McTooth County that he had every intention of upholding the letter of the Law. Order on the other hand did not seem to be one of his primary interests.

The Sheriff's second act of public office was a general distribution of the inventory of seized drugs he found in the safe in his headquarters. First on his list of recipients were the prisoners of the county jail. While he was there he picked out 2 black and 2 white inmates who seemed to possess leadership qualities and made them his deputies.

> Whew! this is a hot mother Jim why don't we make another run by the way what'd you get from Owl Drugs this morning
>
> All they had, Jim said, Bout a thousand tabs, it's in the pick-up
>
> Well, that's pretty good, that'll make a good distribution, uphold one of my policies Take it away from the baboons Round up the Drugs open your eyes Jim Say howd you shoot the incumbent's top teeth out without openin your eyes you shoulda
>
> Fire! McHead spit out, please don't say shoot I despise that word, it's vulgar
>
> *Fire's* what a gun does
>
> Fire?! Not so loud youre gonna move all the customers right outa the chalk see theyre fallin around in there shovin the booths around get outa the way, say Jim have you nailed up the notices telling the brown-loafer and indianhead penny group to leave

beer alone?

Yea I got those up. But they say, George theyre gonna pour that bottle of Schlitz in yor ear.

Fuck those Life-Boy Soap freaks, Ballmik laughed My ear's not where it's gonna go.

Now that I've cleared the cells we'll see what a stretch away from their nasty habits does

Get on the wire Jim and send it out, I want all Impalas shot on sight, soften em up with 12 gauge and then I want 30-ought-30 holes laid across the hoods like they was an artist's conception of the Milky-Way. And get me a report on the promotion of women, pronto, buddyboy.

Can do, Jim muttered and started across the street.

Half way across the street Jim McHead stopped and scratched his head and turned around to fight his way back through the panic stricken crowd from the Chalk making their frenzied hysteric exodus.

And deputize a couple of freaks to put out those Novas, payem off in pills the Sheriff shouted but Jim didn't hear him.

What about the Mustangs? Jim asked, there's gonna be some pressure there, that's a big symbol, the West dig it.

Don't worry about it they're gonna be a special event I'm gonna select some volunteers to drivem straight off the roof of the McEldridge Hotel, that's the highest building in town of any historical connection

Groovey, Jim inserted

Yea that's how I wanta be remembered

Quantrell II and When and If you ever get to the wire check on the chaingang of Leading Businessmen we got breakin that dam apart out on the Platte

Will do, Jim shouted as he tried to stay upright in the swirling crowd.

And get me a report —

Oh shit, Jim muttered as he was spun around Why the fuck did I vote for you

A report on that Detail of Doctors we got fixin the main road

Sheriff Ballmik had his ear to a walkie-talkie

which he held up with his shoulder. He was
wrapping up some low-grade local weed with
one hand while in the palm of the other he
rolled his glass eye around like an agate.

    Here, blow this, Jim said and stuck a
Kazoo in the Sheriff's mouth
The deputy on the other end was shouting god-
damit I can't read you

    He thinks you're givin him something
    to read, George here's your glass eye
    it fell in my boot, now run it down
    again about how much you want the
    county to pay before you'll leave
    the set, Jim asked

    OK here it is and get this on the
Ray at 6 o'clock in front of the news.
I ain't never gonna get off the set
but just to demonstrate how much
this population is overweight they're
gonna have to come up with the
amount of grass that equals their
combined tonnage. In bricks and
neatly stacked. Get that off.

    Right, Jim answered. Anything else.
  Yea goddamit what's that fuckin
Ice Cream Truck doin with the
sireen wide open?

    That's a ambulance George, gimme

a Lucky. What about Fresh Air, Jim asked with a worried look on his face.

Yea, it's about time we got the fuck outa here and got some, the Sheriff answered.

Greene
Arrives on the Set

What birds the fassess bird in the world, you know what I mean, the fassess bird from one place to another, Watch This, which you can't ever see it, fingersnap, like that. What bird would that be? The Fastest Bird the chorus sings, What is the name of the Worlds Swiftest Bird, Yea the fassess, see what I mean? Mr. Dorn whas the name of that bird. Mr. Dorn ducks and his eyes pop out. Several egos swivel their attention and open fire. Mr. Dorn stares at Greene while they run the name up out of the pit. Slow machine guns are that harmless, you can dodge the bullets. The HummingBird! Oh yea the Hummingbird. Thas Right, he moves his wings, up and down, forwards and backwars, an all around 10,000 times in a secunt, and Watch this! hes not even going anywhere, just hittin a few flowers. Greene throws a group of rapid punches around in the air.

Greene arrives on the set. There is no space volunteered by the log. He stands. He computes the scene from the eyes of the audience. All those exposed stalks of the mind tell him he's on, he's the Black Indian, the audience is ready.

He stands. His hair is in good shape. Last week he said Watch this and went to K.C. to keep his appointment with Mr. Cool the anti-astranaut barber. The view from up here is real good, everything going real fine, system functions real well. A chain said to be backed with the money of Jimi Hendrix. He got it pulled out and pushed up into the atmosphere, they gave him a dayglow blue comb with teeth in one end and tines in the other, a design preparing the user for any emergency involving the Hair, or Hunger. The instrument projects from his pocket. On the set at last, Greene speaks.

Greene Speaks. He takes a stance from the assortment gravity has in stock. Greene, Under his theater of hair and out into the orchestra which are his limbs trained then tutored from the ringside Back in Salt Lake City where the bloodfilled mouths of the Pioneers are wiped with golden gloves. There are moments when the sense is so still you can hear a pin drop on the bannister they use for an altar in the tabernacle. He steps straight out of the split world and distributes a cluster of construction sites in the air immediately in front. One angel notices Greene has been stricken from the manifest of existence. Nothing anybody can do about that so it is decided to let the event ride. The Universe is not *that* rich, there arent that many passengers in the coach. Greene Speaks. *Ex Nihilo,* baby. Out of Nothing comes plenty like a mad gravel truck. Bop Whooosh. Up to now weve had cement mixers but theyre not funny anymore. Run two tracks together. Then you realize Faster Than the Speed of Light left town lass week. Greene speaks. I need three women. A slow blues guitar fills the space between the white heads. At the same moment up the hillside of flora and fauna march a troop of Campfire girls toward the spring. They all pretend to conform to the instructions of their leader which were like dont stop and dont look.

Some Business Recently Transacted in the White World

It isn't that easy to get a plane. And availability isn't really the place where they put it. The white world is so dangerous, if you are white, the sheer complication of going into it with a ticket, a handkerchief held at your mouth, a cane to ward off the spectators. A lot of the population hangs around airports these days on the pretense they're going someplace and actually end up with tickets so they won't be caught. Airports are located outside towns so that population won't have to be confronted by a destination. In some way they've bought the right not to be involved. But I didn't get on that way and I didn't catch anything, as much because of my own sureness as any of the precautions I took. In New Mexico the colored man still holds the door but fuck that who asked him. I don't want to be bothered by that either.

What I did can only be *thought* permanent, cannot have permanence. We go through that like a verb through sense. If you remember it, that way, as a concrete act the mistake is twofold. The nature of *it* is twofold. That's surely the heaviest *isolated* problem the white world is going to avoid whether it wants to or not, not color. That assumes itself, it isn't up to *anybody*. Color is an attribute of the character. Commonplace. More on the acquisition of something a century later when it can be looked at. There are certain aspects present which should be left as all over. Finished in the definitions they've acquired spread uniformly across time. Concrete time flows out the hole of a mixer truck around a cornerstone with some unknown local Christian's name trying to get fixed on it. It's going to have the retentive power of an icecube. A time capsule which when broken open will reveal the man inside turned into the name his chums called him from the simple frustration of being unable to think of something else. New York. Or you can forget the debt and call it Boston. I can't quite deal with the man who remembers to speak my name alongside a load of other matter about me he's trying hard to forget. A white man, any man who makes himself white discovers spirit he covers himself with the ashes of the blowing sign of the universe, local materials. The population has managed to embarrass itself enough to forget that too. On the turf inside the Racetrack there are still a few jockeys of refusal. The spare numerical presentations we are. We are of the end of the leeching which produced us. A spoonful left at the bottom, very refined, pure stuff, the final dry powder, the dust that lives. The crack it will go into, the crack in the real. The quality is obvious to everyone though of course like quality it can be faked as some revival called a revolution. It isn't automatic by living that you get your own song. But if you want it off your back, if you want to, turn the scab off, the social off.

In the first days of the horse of December crossing Barcelona in those taxis she had something literal to do, when she could speak in a picked up tongue, learn how it's done with a new monkey wrench, sharp teeth, wieldable. The light traveled from behind her eyes like spirit flashes and focused on the thing to be shone. My function was to be there, pay the cabbie, say muchas gracias, keep my fingers out of slammed doors and smile like I knew what was up, the useful, respectable function machines have when they feel good. That was it. But the highest kind of help is simply handwork. That was occasionally possible. Opening the closed. It may not be as exciting as jumping around but that depends on what's inside. Some figures must be given a sum to find. Their growth is based somewhat on a variation of finding the thimble in the universe. He, on the other hand was not of routine birth, came in differently as a piece of luck, from a conception sprung. So he has his life, others just notice what they think he is. Now is now, like it was then. If there is something called man, which is used to mean *mean* unless it's in a picture book, if there is something of the animal still in man it might be interesting to see what that is before killing it with a request to remember what Happened.